A Friend in Need!

Illustrated by Kate Pankhurst

by Julia Jarman

Andersen Press · London

First published in 2013 by
Andersen Press Limited
20 Vauxhall Bridge Road
London SW1V 2SA
www.andersenpress.co.uk

2 4 6 8 10 9 7 5 3

ISBN 978 1 84939 576 2

Printed and bound in Great Britain
by CPI Group UK (Ltd), Croydon, CR0 4YY

For Hattie and Phoebe, great nieces!

Daisy is friendly and gets on with everyone. She's kind and sensible. She's always thinking of how she can help others and loves being a school 'buddy'. She hates it when people fall out and was very upset when her parents split up, though she's got used to it now.

Phoebe is shy and finds it hard to make friends. She enjoys craft which she can do on her own – but it's even better with Daisy. And Daisy shares her love of reading. She likes the peace and quiet of Daisy's house, where they can get on without being disturbed by Phoebe's little brothers, The Smellies.

Erika is entertaining. She's full of energy and very sporty. She means well but sometimes doesn't realise she's hurting people's feelings. She tries very hard to please her parents who expect her to be good at everything, and sometimes that's a strain.

Erika

Thursday

Daisy

Erika's not talking to me.

At school I put a note in her drawer saying, 'What's the matter? PLEASE let's talk.' But she didn't answer. And I've just texted, 'Shall I come round?' But she hasn't texted back.

Perhaps she didn't find my note? Actually, I didn't see her go to her drawer before the bell went and she had to rush off to a match or race, or something.

Maybe I'm worrying too much.

But Erika's not talking to Phoebe, either. And Phoebe isn't answering my texts. I know she thinks I'm worrying too much about Erika, but Phoebe doesn't know Erika like I do. They didn't used to get on, but I've sorted that out. We've all been friends for weeks now.

Now it looks as if they've both gone off *me*. So I'm stuck in my bedroom with no one to talk to except Marmalade, and he's fast asleep. Mum's downstairs but she'd just tell me not to worry if I told her. I suppose I could go round Phoebe's, but what if Erika comes here while I'm there?

The reason I'm worried about Erika is that I think she's in some sort of trouble. She's been acting really strangely. But why won't she tell me what it is? I wouldn't tell anyone – well not unless she's in *danger*. I wouldn't even tell Phoebe if Erika didn't want me to. Although that would upset Phoebe if she found out. But I'm really trustworthy and sensible. Everyone says so. That's why I'm a school buddy.

Oh, dear. How am I going to find out what's bugging Erika? I hate it when we're not speaking.

Phoebe

I'm fed up with Daisy going on and on about Erika. It's all she ever talks – or texts – about at the moment. And we're only supposed to use our new mobiles for emergencies.

Erika really hurt my feelings today. I took in my spare Moshi cards to do a swap and she didn't even look at them. She just looked as if she'd been turned into a horrible Glump and went off to practise shooting at goal. That's probably what it's about in fact. When Erika's got a match coming up it's bye-bye to her non-sporty friends till it's all over. She's SO sporty!

Oh no, here's another text from Daisy.

MUST FIND WHATS UP WTH E

Why? It's not a mystery. Erika's good fun except when she's got a race or a match or a tournament. Then she's just BORING. It's train train train.

I'm texting Daisy.

PLEASE CAN WE GET ON WTH OUR PROJECT?

We're designing a set for our next show at Drama Club, *The Thwarting of Baron Bollingrew*. I've got this cardboard box which will make a great medieval castle IF – quick, close door! – I can get it to Daisy's before my little brothers wreck it. That's another thing, Erika's decided not to be in this show. And we really need her because there are fifteen parts and only twelve of us to act them, as well as all the men at arms and poor and needy villagers. Erika would make a great Mike Magpie. I can just see her hopping all over the stage making everyone laugh. Daisy thinks so too, so we're both going to text her and say she's GOT to be in it.

Oh no, more trouble. The Smellies are bawling their heads off. Enter Mum any moment now to blame me. Honestly, nothing's going right at the moment.

Erika

Oh, dear. I know I'm upsetting Dais and Phoebe, but what else can I do? I've got to deal with this myself. But if I see Dais and Phoebe I'll blab, I know I will. It will all come pouring out and they'll start treating me like some poor little kid who's fallen over in the playground.

I can hear Daisy now. 'You're being *bullied*, Erika!'

No, Dais, I'm NOT! It's just some stupid person trying to scare me off winning.

AND Daisy would insist we tell a teacher which would make things a trillion zillion times worse. I mean it's most likely someone just joking. They'd laugh their heads off if I made a fuss about it. Me? Bullied? I don't think so. I'm not a wimpy loser and I'm absolutely not scared by a few texts. The thing to do is keep quiet, play it cool. Then they won't even know if I'm getting the texts.

But I really wish I knew who was sending them. Trouble is the cowardy custard is hiding SENT BY. How do they do that? And how have they got my number? Oh no, here's another one.

YR NOT LIST-NIN R U?

That must be because I won all my heats tonight. I'm fastest in the county! And here's another.

OK. LET U OF THIS TIME
BUT LOOSE 3 SHYRES

Aha! A clue! The creep can't spell. AND they want to win the Three Counties' Cross Country even more than I do. But, no, that's not a clue. Everyone wants to win. I mean, why run if you don't? Well, whoever the creep is they don't know me if they think a few texts can scare me off! I'm going for a run right now.

'Come on, Rolly!'

But better text Daisy first. Super-sensitive Dais has sensed something's wrong so I'll just say everything's hunky dory.

**NOTHING UP JUST FOCUSSED
ON RACE. C U IN MORNING.**

'Come on, Rolly. Wake up. We're in training!'

Friday

Daisy

Phew! Panic over. Last night I had a cheery text from Erika – saying she's in training for the cross country finals. So, Phoebe's right, that's why she's been a bit off lately. It's not because she's avoiding us. She's just focussed on her running.

Phoebe's still grumpy though. I went round hers last night and she said Erika should think of other people more, but I can see why Erika doesn't want to be in the Drama Club show. This is a really big race for her.

Anyway, I think I managed to cheer Phoebe up. We got on with the model of the set. Then we had a bit of a clothes swap. I lent Phoebe my sparkly pumps and she lent me her new skirt. And I brought the model home with me to keep it safe from the Smellies.

Oh, Marmalade's woken up. I thought I heard a dog barking. 'It's OK, Marmalade, it's only Erika and Rolly and he's nice to cats.' He's on one of those long leads anyway. They're running past our house. Well Erika is, she's miles ahead! Poor old Rolly obviously wants to stop, but she doesn't.

Erika didn't even wave. Never mind. We're still friends, that's the main thing, and when this race is over, we'll get back to normal.

Drama Club tonight – my fave night of the week! I'd better get round to Phoebe's as her mum's taking us.

Erika

'Well, Rolly, didn't today go well? Think I deserve an Oscar after today's performance. Dais and Phoebe were well taken in, and if Secret Sender was watching he or she would be well miffed to see me so upbeat. I didn't see anyone at school giving me evil looks so I'm pretty sure it isn't anyone there. No more texts today so SS must have got the message – DON'T MESS WITH ERIKA!

'This is just between you and me, Rolly. Luckily I can tell you anything, or I'd burst, but I'm sure it's best not to tell the others. Sometimes I think you're the cuddliest-wuddliest best friend I've got. Sorry, though, I've got to leave you here tomorrow morning as I'm running with Mum. She thinks I should step up the training and says you slow me down.'

Better get some sleep now. Oh, here's another text!

**PLEASE PLEASE PLEASE
BE IN THE PLAY, E!!!**

Phew! It's from Daisy. And here's another.

NOT SAME WITHOUT YOU!!!

That's Phoebe. They must have just got back from Drama Club.

OH, I hate disappointing them but I really really have to put *everything* I've got into winning the Three Counties. Mum says there might be *national* coaches there and if I win they may select me to run for the *country*, or at least join their training sessions. I mean, I could be heading for the next Olympics! That's better than a poxy play.

**SORRY GIRLS GOT MORE
IMPORTANT THINGS TO DO!!!**

Saturday

Phoebe

I can't believe what Erika texted last night. There I was really missing her and telling her so. Then we got that rude message back. Now I'm glad she's not going to be in the play. We'll manage without her. Erika's not just rude, she's insulting. But Daisy doesn't seem to mind! She says Erika's being jokey and that I haven't got a sense of humour and that's the big difference between Erika and me, and the sooner I get a sense of humour the better.

Cheek!

When she came round this afternoon I said, 'Daisy, please tell me why does Erika think what she's doing is more important than what we're doing?' And Daisy sighed dramatically and said, 'She doesn't, not really. It was a joke. J-O-K-E.'

She says Erika is always joking and the thing to do is joke back. I said I think we should ignore her but Daisy's texting Erika now.

YOULL BE SORRY IF YOU DON'T!!!

I said, 'What are you going to do to her if she doesn't?'

And she rolled her eyes and said, 'Nothing of course, I'm J-O-K-I-N-G.'

Sometimes those two make me feel really left out.

Erika

A text from Dais! What does she mean though? YOULL BE SORRY IF YOU DON'T!!!

That doesn't sound friendly.

And here's another.

GLAD U LEFT MUT BEHIND

What does she mean by that? Oh no, this one's not from Dais. It's from Secret Sender! Or – just had a thought – I mean could Daisy BE the secret sender? Could Daisy and Phoebe both be? Whoever it is saw me running with Rolly yesterday and then without Rolly today, when I went running with Mum, and I do run past Daisy's house. Yes! It must be her. It's obvious. She must have just forgotten to delete sender with that 'YOU'LL BE SORRY' one. So that's it! Mystery solved! Phew! Dais's miffed because I've dropped out of Drama Club and because I'm not doing stuff with her and Phoebe all the time. So I was right all along. It *is* a joker, but only Dais. Double phew! I'm so glad I didn't make a fuss. She'd have laughed her head off.

And here's another. Oh, now she's going too far.

LOOSE RASE OR WILL GET YR MUT

Does she really think that's funny? Well, I don't. It's horrible. No one threatens Rolly and gets away with it. Daisy had better look out!

Monday

Phoebe

Daisy and Erika have had a terrible bust-up. Erika was waiting by the gate when we got to school and she just flew at Daisy.

'How could you? How could you?' She *screamed*.

Daisy said, 'It was a joke, Erika.'

'Some joke! Threatening Rolly!' Then Erika stormed off into the playground where all the sporty girls gathered round. Next thing they're all looking daggers at Daisy, who's mystified.

Daisy was in a right state. Obviously her little joke misfired, but she didn't know what Erika was on about, about threatening Rolly I mean. Nor did I. Daisy hadn't threatened Rolly. Daisy would never do anything like that. But someone must have. And because Daisy sent her jokey YOU'LL BE SORRY IF YOU DON'T text, Erika thought it was her.

Well, I decided I'd talk to Erika, after I'd tried to get Daisy to calm down. I'd never seen her so upset or so negative. She's the one who's always telling me off for being negative, but she was saying that we couldn't work it out if Erika wouldn't talk to us. Daisy was sure Erika would never ever talk to her again. She was devastated that Erika could even *think* she'd threaten Rolly.

I managed to get Daisy to stop crying before we went into school and at break she was on buddy duty in the infants' playground. So I went to find Erika by myself – hoping she wouldn't see me shaking in my shoes, well Daisy's sparkly pumps.

Honestly, though, I was nervous. Erika can be shouty.

I found her by the scooter park with some of her other friends, most of the netball team, and she said, 'I'm not talking to you, Pheeble, not if you're still friends with *her*.'

She used to call me Pheeble before we became friends.

I could see Daisy in the infants' playground and so could Erika. I think she'd been watching her. Anyway I took a deep breath and came right out with it.

'You've got it all wrong, Erika. Daisy sent you one text as a joke.' And I explained what had happened.

Erika didn't look convinced, but then her

mobile went *ping*. Another text. She read it, looked across at Daisy, and frowned.

'What does it say?' I asked. She showed it to me.

NOT JOCKING LOOSE
3C OR DOG GETS IT

I said, 'That wasn't Daisy, Daisy can spell. And look at her.' But I didn't need to. Erika could see Daisy playing hopscotch with some little kids. Her mobile was nowhere in sight.

'W-who was it then?' Her voice was a sort of trembly mumble. I think she was upset and a bit ashamed. 'Th-that's the second time they've threatened him.'

I said, 'Who has?'

'Don't know, do I?' she snapped, stroppy Erika now. 'That's the trouble. The creep deletes SENT BY. If I knew who it was I'd go right round and get them. I'd, I'd—'

Another text came in and she showed it to me.

WE NO U R READIN THIS

Someone was watching us – and texting. It was a really weird feeling. We both looked around the playground then to see who it might be – but I couldn't see anyone with a mobile, though they could be hiding it.

Daisy was staring at us now.

I wanted to beckon her over, but said, 'What does 3C mean?'

'Three Counties,' Erika wailed. 'Someone

wants me to lose the Three Counties Cross-Country finals at the end of the month. But what do they mean by "the dog gets it"?'

I could see from her face that she was picturing something horrible being done to Rolly.

I said, 'No one would hurt Rolly, Erika. I mean, you couldn't.'

Honestly, I'm not particularly doggy, but when Rolly looks at me with his big soulful eyes I can feel myself going all ah-ish.

'*You* couldn't,' she said. 'And . . . Daisy couldn't, but some people are cruel.'

I took that as my cue to call Daisy over and we had a group hug with lots of sorries, then Erika told us the whole story. It had started five days ago with a text SLO DOWN OR ELS just before the County Cross Country final.

'Since then they've got nastier.' She showed us the texts.

Daisy said, 'Erika, this is serious. We've got

to tell a grown-up.'

Erika grabbed Daisy's arm. 'NO, Dais! Don't!'

Then the bell rang and I said, 'Let's keep it to ourselves for the mo and talk about it again at dinner. Meanwhile let's all keep watch and see if we can find out who texted WE NO U R READIN THIS. It must be someone in school.

'There's no need to panic. It's two weeks to the Three Counties race. I know we'll be able to work it out before then.'

Erika

I feel better for telling Dais and Phoebe – and finding out that Secret Sender wasn't Dais. I don't know how I could have thought it really. Just shows what a state I was in. Phoebe's right – I've got to keep calm. Just hope Dais doesn't blab to a teacher.

There would probably be an assembly about it and I'd look a complete idiot. *Ha ha, Erika's being bullied.* And Mrs Davies would tell Mum who'd charge in fists flying and SS would dive for cover and we'd never find out.

Actually, this is worse than bullying, it's blackmail, and the important thing is to FIND OUT WHO'S DOING THIS. For Rolly's sake.

I'm going to watch everyone in class very carefully.

Daisy

It's maths and there's a lot of watching going on. Some of Erika's other friends are giving me hard stares. Erika's being a bit obvious staring at one person for about a minute and then moving on to the next. She isn't concentrating on the lesson at all, which is unusual for her. Her hand's usually up and down like a yoyo.

And someone else is watching her. Callum. Mind you, he never concentrates in lessons. Miss Perkins is always shouting at him to get on with his work. But he's concentrating now – on Erika. But why? He's not even a runner.

Actually several people are watching Erika, probably wondering what's wrong with her. She's acting so out of character. I think watching isn't enough. We need a real plan of action.

Tuesday

Phoebe

Daisy's turned detective! She thinks we can solve this mystery, but I think we should just tell a grown-up.

I mean by not telling we could be putting Rolly's life in DANGER. Why doesn't Erika want to tell anyone? What's wrong with saying you're being bullied? I suppose Erika thinks she'll look like a loser, but it's better than being bullied.

Anyway, Detective Daisy had this plan for both of us to go to Athletics Club with Erika, to one of her training sessions, tonight. But I didn't think my mum would let me, and she didn't. So Daisy's gone by herself, well, with Erika, who's told her mum that Daisy wants to cheer her on. But Daisy's really going to watch all the other runners to see who's desperate to win. She thinks if she finds someone who

34

wants to win even more than Erika does it might be the secret sender. I said look at the parents too and see if any of them shout louder than Erika's mum.

Mum wouldn't let me go because she wanted me to help with the Smellies at bath time.

They're being little horrors at the mo, even worse than usual. I was brill with them so at least I'm in Mum's good books, but I can't help wondering how Daisy's getting on.

Daisy

It was boring and exhausting! *I* had to run! Erika's mum insisted. It wouldn't have been so bad if Erika was one of the sprinters. They hung around a lot between races, but cross country is all about stamina so they run for ages. I don't know how many circuits I did but I'm sure I ran a marathon. It wasn't even a race, just training, but Erika was way ahead of the others all the way and she put this spurt on at the end and everyone cheered. I could hear them, even though I was miles behind.

When I got off the track I tried to tune in to what people were saying – after I got my breath back – but I only heard praise for Erika, except from her mum. She had this huge stop watch and kept saying that Erika's time was actually rather slow and she needed someone to challenge her.

It seems Ashley, the boy who usually does, was away.

I'm beginning to think this plan won't work, either. I mean, everyone seemed really happy for Erika, except her mum, but her mum wouldn't send her threatening texts.

At least I can see why Erika likes Athletics Club. She's really popular there. There's a team of four running in the Three Counties and two of the others were there – one girl, one boy – but Erika was definitely the star.

I think we need a different tactic. I'm going to ask Phoebe. She's the one with the clever ideas.

Thursday

Erika

Phoebe thinks I should tell the POLICE! So does Daisy! Typical! I knew those two would go OTT. I should never have told them. I've forbidden them of course – to tell *anyone* – but Phoebe had this 'brilliant' idea that the police could hack into the phone, find out who's threatening me and go round and sort them out. Well, that would be great except that *everyone* would know!

Actually, it's three days since the last text so it looks like Secret Sender has given up. Oh, I really can't waste any more time on this. I've got to concentrate on winning. Mum will go ballistic if I don't improve my times. I run faster when I have someone to pace myself against so I asked Ashley to come round tonight.

When I rang him his dad answered and he sounded horrible. I heard him call out, 'Your girlfriend wants to put you through your paces, Ash. Are you up to it?'

No wonder Ashley sounded nervous, but he said he thought meeting up and running together was a great idea. He said he needed

to get back in training because he's had a bug and been off for a few days. That's why he missed Tuesday night.

Only one drawback, Rolly will have to come with us. I don't see how else I can manage to take him for a walk and fit in netball practice after school. Just hope I don't have to keep stopping to fill poo-bags. That would be SO embarrassing.

'No poos, Rolly!'

Friday

Phoebe

Callum's definitely watching Erika. He hardly lets her out of his sight. And it's not just in school. When I told Daisy I was sure he was looking at Erika in school she punched the air as if she'd just won the lottery. She'd noticed it too. We really are super sleuths!

Another thing – I checked Callum's spelling. It's awful.

The question is: *why is he watching her?* Anyway we decided to try and see if he watches her outside of school as well. First we hung around at home-time and observed he went off in the same direction as Erika usually does, though she didn't last night because of netball. Daisy said he lives quite near Erika, so he could follow her easily. She used to live at that end too.

On the way home Daisy and I discussed the

all-important *why*. I said, 'Daisy, you don't think Callum could, like, *love* Erika do you?'

Daisy said, 'Boys in our year do not love *girls*, Phoebe. They love football, computer games, and possibly designer trainers but girls NO.'

But later on Daisy texted me:

LOOK OUT OF WINDOW!!!

Daisy

I could hardly believe it – not just Erika and Rolly running by with a boy I didn't know, but also Callum, *lurking.* Following them. I'm sure of it, because though he was looking in the window of the paper-shop, pretending to read the notices, once they'd passed he set off after them lickety-split. Phoebe texted seconds later to say she'd seen first them, then him, go past her house.

Of course Phoebe thinks this proves Callum's in love with Erika, but I still don't. There must be some other reason.

Today we told Erika what we'd noticed and of course asked her who she was running with. She said it was the boy from the Athletics Club who was missing on Tuesday night. His name's Ashley and he's her closest rival and

they're training together blah blah blah. She went on and on about times and stuff till Phoebe yawned rather pointedly.

Phoebe said, 'Erika, he, this Ashley, he couldn't be the one who's threatening you, could he?' But Erika said, 'Thought of that and no. First he's nice; second we're both in the same team and want to win; third he was friendly to Rolly. Besides, all that's stopped now.'

'For the moment,' said Phoebe. 'And, this Ashley, he could just be pretending to be nice as a cover.'

Then Phoebe told Erika about Callum. 'He's following you round like a dog. It's creepy.'

But Erika just shrugged. 'He's probably just one of my fan-club.'

Honestly, I can see why she drives Phoebe mad sometimes.

But if Erika's not going to look out for herself we've got to look out for her.

Monday

Phoebe

In the playground this morning Daisy asked Callum straight out what he was up to. He said, 'Dunno what you mean,' and went bright red.

Then Erika breezed over. 'Leave him alone, you two!' Next thing she was chatting away to him about this Ashley and how great he was and how Saturday morning training had gone really well and how she and Ashley had improved their times. Blah blah.

YAWN!

Daisy went over to the infants' playground to sort out two little kids who were fighting, and I went to the loo.

When we were back in class Erika came and wrapped her arms round our shoulders. 'Thanks for trying to help, you guys, but – how many times do I have to tell you? – there's no need.' She whispered, 'No you-know-whats for days now, and – mystery solved – Callum is Ashley's cousin.'

She said she'd told Ashley about Callum, and he said it wasn't *her* Callum was following, but *him*. He was really embarrassed and said Callum had always sort of hero-worshipped him.

She obviously thought she'd explained away everything, but she didn't see what I saw a few minutes later.

Daisy

Phoebe says Callum was texting in class. Well, she saw his hand in his pocket. I said, 'So? That doesn't prove anything.' She said he got one back almost immediately. She heard it *ping*. I said that still doesn't prove anything. She said, 'It must have been important for him to text in class and risk getting his phone confiscated.'

At packed lunches we asked Erika if she'd had any texts and she rolled her eyes. 'NO, because one – we're not allowed to have our mobiles on in class, remember, and two – I told you, that's all stopped!' She showed us her empty inbox.

Then I asked her what she'd talked to Callum about when we'd gone and she said, 'Stuff that wouldn't interest you two. Sporty stuff.'

I said, 'I'm interested. It's Phoebe who isn't.'

Erika sighed dramatically then said, 'Mainly Ashley, if you must know, and how his dad will give him a hard time if he doesn't win. He said if he's beaten by a girl he'll never hear the end of it.'

Phoebe said '*Mmm*' and nodded as if she'd spotted an important clue, which made Erika snort. 'It's not what you're thinking. Ashley wouldn't threaten Rolly. '

Phoebe said, 'I was only going to say Callum's trying to make you feel sorry for Ashley, to slow you down.'

'Slow me down?' Erika looked at her as if she was mad.

But when Erika rang me after school she was HYSTERICAL.

Erika

ROLLY HAS GONE!!!!

When I got home from school he wasn't there. We walked in – Mum, me and my two brothers – and the house was very quiet, which was unusual. Rolly usually starts throwing himself at the door when he hears us. Well, at first I thought he must be in the garden because Mum leaves him there sometimes when she comes to pick me up from school, but when I went outside he wasn't there!

I started to worry. Then I thought Dad had taken him for a walk till I realised Dad's car wasn't there. Then I yelled, 'Mum, Rolly's gone!' in total panic and she yelled back, 'He must have escaped again!'

Well, he did have a phase of getting out of the garden when he was smaller and before Dad put up wire netting behind the hedge. Mum came out to the garden, but she seemed more annoyed than worried and said we'd look for him later, when she'd got the tea in the oven. But she doesn't know what I know, so I rang Dais.

Next thing Dais is banging on the door. She'd whizzed round on her bike and went straight into detective mode. It must be all those books she reads. Soon we're in the back garden on our hands and knees examining the hedge at the back. Dais found the hole. Someone had cut through the wire netting.

It was obvious, though they'd tried to pull the edges together to cover the gap.

'They must have had wire clippers,' said Daisy. 'You have to be quite strong to make them work. And they've broken some branches so I think this is the work of a grown-up or a strong teenager.'

I found some of Rolly's lovely woolly hair clinging to the broken branches as if he'd been dragged through and have to admit I started crying. By this time I was frantic. Mum must have been watching through the kitchen

window because she came out and when she saw the hole she zoomed into action. Well, after she'd got the boys back in the garden. They'd charged through the hole onto the road at the back. Mum rang the police straightaway. I thought they'd zoom round in a police car but they didn't.

We waited and waited but they didn't come. Mum said lost dogs – even stolen dogs – aren't a priority for the hard-pressed police force, especially if the dog isn't a pedigree. She said, 'Rolly isn't valuable, Erika.'

I said, 'He is to me! He's priceless!'

Then I blurted out about the threats and everything and she rang the police again. Mum says I mustn't let this affect my performance, to leave it to her, she'll sort it, but I've decided what I'm going to do. NOT do. I'm NOT going to run and I'm going to make sure everyone knows. All I want to do is get Rolly back.

Tuesday

Phoebe

I feel really sorry for Erika. She's frantic. She really does love Rolly more than she loves winning. I sometimes had my doubts about that, but Daisy says she knew all along that Erika had a heart. She just doesn't show it sometimes.

I think the only reason Erika came to school today was to tell everyone she wasn't going to run in the Three Counties Final. Her eyes were all red from crying. She said she'd texted everyone she could in the Athletics Club too. In the dinner hour we made loads of LOST DOG notices, offering a big reward to the finder. Miss Perkins let us stay in. Erika says she's going to put her bike on eBay to get the money. Daisy and I are doing everything we can to help. We're all going to put the notices up after school.

Trouble is some people are making Erika feel worse. She got loads of texts back from people in the Athletics Club saying she has to think of the team not herself. But she's not thinking of herself, she's thinking of Rolly.

Even Mrs Davies says she thinks Erika should run, and of course her mum does. They both say it's wrong to give in to blackmailers because it encourages them.

Mrs Davies gave an assembly about it and said that anybody who knew anything about Rolly should go and tell her. I watched Callum who looked at his feet all the time. I'm sure he knows something. I mean *who is he texting and who's texting him?*

I want to follow him home tonight – and see if he meets anyone. He might even lead us to Rolly. We could do it because Erika's mum has invited us to tea and to Athletics Club afterwards. Erika doesn't want to go, but her mum says she's got to. And Daisy has persuaded Erika to go – she said we might get more clues – so Erika's mum thinks we're on her side.

Daisy

Callum walked home – well as far as Erika's – with us, so Phoebe's plan was scuppered. But she's still convinced Callum's trying to put Erika off running because he wants Ashley to win. She also thinks he knows something about the Rolly-napping, but he sounded all sympathetic when we talked about it, and said he hoped she'd find Rolly at home when she got there.

I'm not sure.

Rolly wasn't at home. Callum came in with us and Erika showed him the hole in the hedge. Poor Erika looks awful, as if she hasn't slept since Rolly went, but I'd be the same if it was Marmalade.

When Callum left, Phoebe waited a few seconds then shot off after him. I knew she was going to follow him – to see if he led her to Rolly – but I thought it would look odd if we both went so I said let's examine the hole again.

Erika and I climbed through easily, so I'm convinced it was someone tall. In the lane at the back I noticed tyre marks in the mud at the side, as if a car was parked there recently. So we're probably looking for someone who can drive.

Phoebe came back while I was trying to work out how to take a photo of the tyre marks on my mobile.

Phoebe

Daisy's very excited about the tyre marks, but what does she want us to do? Go round examining car tyres? Matching them up? There could be thousands of cars with tyres like that. I said, 'Daisy, you're not Miss Marple.'

'Have you got a better idea?' she asked.

Trouble is, I haven't.

The Callum trail led nowhere, well only to his house, so before he went in I came out of hiding and asked him straight out, 'Where's Rolly?' He made that screw loose sign and said, 'How do I know?' I said, 'There's no need to be rude, Callum, I know you're trying to put Erika off so that Ashley beats her. That isn't fair, you know.'

He went red then, but shouted, 'I don't know where her daft mutt is! If I knew I'd tell you!'

I don't know if I believe him.

Erika is hoping Rolly will just turn up now she's said she's not running. She thinks the dognappers will let him go.

Daisy said, 'Sorry, Erika, but I don't think they will let him go just because you've *said* you won't run. They'll wait till after the race and see if you keep your word.'

'But that's a whole week away!' Erika started crying again.

Erika

Rolly hates being away from home unless I'm with him, or at least someone in our family is. When we go away on holiday my gran comes to stay with him. We put him in kennels once, just for a weekend, and he refused to eat. What if he hasn't eaten for days? He could pine away completely!

Another thing, Mum says I've got to go to the track tonight. Well, I'll go but I'm NOT running. I don't care what she or anyone says. If someone's spying they'll see I'm not running. I know I'm giving in to blackmail, but what else can I do?

wednesday

Daisy

Last night at the track I was really proud of Erika. She refused to run even though her mum was furious. Several people came up and said, 'Think of the team' and stuff like that but Erika wouldn't give in.

Ashley looked miserable. He ran round the track but as if he had heavy weights tied to his feet. When he came in nearly last his dad looked as if he might hit him, but this girl with a scary haircut and nose-ring – I'd say she was about sixteen – said, 'Cool it, Dad. He hasn't recovered his form yet, that's all.'

But that wasn't all. At school today Callum said to Erika that Ashley had told his dad that he wouldn't run if Erika didn't, and his dad went ballistic and locked him in his room.

Erika said, 'Tell him to run. Tell him I said so. I don't want him getting into trouble on my behalf.' And Callum said, 'Thanks, Erika, that's what we hoped you'd say, but can you sort of put it in writing so he knows?'

Phoebe put her face really close to his and said, 'We? You said "That's what we hoped you'd say." So who's putting you up to this? Who's "we"?'

Callum went red then and said, 'Er, Ashley and me, of course.'

Phoebe said, 'I don't believe you. You'd better tell us the truth, Callum, or I'm going to tell everyone you've got a crush on Erika. Everyone's noticed you've been following her around.'

It was a brilliant tactic. Callum spilled straightaway. 'Lynne, Ashley's big sister. It's just because she's worried about him.'

Neither of us asked if she'd been sending the threatening texts, or more importantly, if she'd dognapped Rolly but we're pretty sure it must be her.

At break Erika wrote a note to Ashley and gave it to Callum.

Phoebe and I think we're getting warm, but what do we do next?

Erika

Ashley's just phoned to say thanks for the note but he still doesn't want to run, because he THINKS HIS SISTER LYNNE HAS BEEN SENDING ME THREATENING TEXTS!

He heard her talking to her boyfriend about it. He said not to blame her because he's sure she was trying to help. And she's always looked out for him since his mum died. But then his phone went all funny and I couldn't hear anything. Oh, poor Ashley, I didn't know he hadn't got a mum. But that doesn't help me find Rolly. Or does it?

I rang straight back to say ASK HER WHERE ROLLY IS!!! But there was no answer. His phone must have run out of battery.

I really really want to go straight round his house but I'm feeling awful. I don't know if

73

it's because I'm frantic with worry about Rolly or I've got that bug Ashley had. Probably both. Oh no, I've got to go to the loo again!

I know what I'll do – text Daisy.

Thursday

Phoebe

We're on the trail!

Erika's not at school today, but she phoned Daisy this morning begging us both to help find Rolly because she was feeling too ill. Seems she can't risk not being near a toilet. *I* think we should go the police now we've got more evidence, but Daisy's gone into Miss Marple mode – triple! She's taken a photo of the tyre-track prints and says we should go round Ashley's house, and see if there's a car outside. If there is and if the tyre marks match we should wait till someone gets in it and follow them.

I asked her, 'HOW, Daisy? On our bikes?'

She said, 'Well at least we can find out which direction they're going in.'

I was about to say, 'OK then,' when someone yelled, 'It's snowing!' and everyone rushed to the window including Miss Perkins. It's not fair. We should be thinking about building a snowman after school or having a snowball fight, not looking for horrible dognappers. But we've got to try. Rolly's been missing for four days now and if he hasn't been eating . . . It's too awful to think about.

Anyway, I have agreed to go with Daisy to Ashley's house after school so Daisy can try her matching tyre marks idea – if there's a car outside – but first I've got to get Callum to tell me Ashley's address.

I feel a bit bad because we've told our mums we're going to take a get well-card to Erika. Still, if we do that afterwards it won't be a fib and we might have some good news about Rolly.

Daisy

Phoebe got Ashley's address from Callum easy-peasy, along with desperate pleas not to drop him in it. She said Callum seemed dead scared of Ashley's big sister, so we approached the house warily.

It took us about ten minutes to get there. Number 22 Meadway is an oldish house on an estate and it looks a bit scruffy. Luckily, though, it's on a corner and there's a hedge in front of it so we had two places to hide. But there wasn't a car outside. Phoebe wanted to leave right then, but I persuaded her to wait a bit, to see if a car would come. Then something even better happened!

First we saw Ashley looking out of an upstairs window, and he saw us and started waving, no not waving I realised at last, but pointing – downwards.

Then we saw why – the front door opened and his sister came out carrying a plastic bag that looked quite heavy though not very full. A tin of dog food? Possibly, from the way it thumped against her leg.

Well, we scooted round the corner to hide and watch. Which direction would she go in? Oh no! Towards the road we were hiding in! But we got behind a post-box just before she walked right past the end of the road. Then we set off after her, hoping she wouldn't turn round. Mind you, we had our hoods pulled up and our heads down.

Lynne strode along as if she knew where she was going. After about five minutes we saw a primary school, St Asaph's – Erika had told us that's where Ashley goes – and then some allotments surrounded by railings. Lynne slowed down and Phoebe touched my arm and I knew what she was thinking because I had the same thought.

There were sheds dotted all over the allotments. Rolly could be in one of them. There weren't many people about. In fact the allotments were deserted as they must have been all winter. I was thinking that no one would have heard poor Rolly if he had been howling when Phoebe's grip tightened.

Lynne had stopped at a gate.

We stopped and pressed ourselves against the railings.

Lynne looked round then opened the gate.

Our plan was to stay out of sight and watch, just watch and find out where Rolly was so we could rescue him later.

But our plan went wrong.

Phoebe

We were pressed against the railings when a car drew up and a HUGE teenager got out!

He yelled, 'Lynne!'

She turned round still holding the gate and the giant teenager started coming towards US. 'D'ya know these two scags?'

Well, of course we ran, and Daisy got away, but he grabbed hold of my arm.

'What two?' Lynne came running up. 'What are you doing, idiot? Let her go.'

'This girl, these girls . . . they were spying on you. They've been following you. Look.' He pointed to our footprints in the snow.

I said, 'We were coming to the allotments. That's all.' I looked round desperately though I hoped that didn't show. 'To pick some Brussel sprouts for our mum.'

Brussel sprouts were about the only things I could see growing.

Lynne stared at me. 'Do I know you?'

I shrugged and shook my head and hoped she didn't recognise me from my one visit to the track.

'What about the other one?' said Giant Teenager.

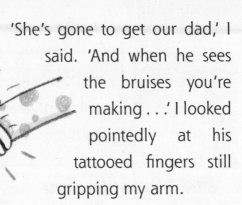

'She's gone to get our dad,' I said. 'And when he sees the bruises you're making . . .' I looked pointedly at his tattooed fingers still gripping my arm.

Lynne said, 'I told you to let her go. Come *on*.' She was standing by the car. 'Come ON!'

Reluctantly he let go. Then they both got into the car. They both swore when it didn't start straightaway and I held my breath. I was shaking. It seemed ages before the car spluttered into action and they roared off in a cloud of exhaust smoke.

Now what? It was beginning to get dark, snow was falling again and the place was deserted. *Should I start searching the huts all by myself for Rolly or try and find my way home?*

Daisy

Phoebe didn't know that I was watching. I was hiding in the school yard texting and phoning desperately. Trouble is I didn't get any answers. No one replied. So much for having mobiles to use in emergencies!

As soon as the car roared off I came out of hiding and yelled, 'Phoebe!' I made my way as fast as I could to her, slipping and sliding on the snowy path.

'What happened?' I gasped. 'How did you get rid of them? You were brilliant!'

Phoebe looked as if she was going to cry. 'Rolly, I'm sure he's in one of those sheds.'

I nodded, I could tell Phoebe was longing to go home and I didn't blame her – she must have been terrified. But I said, 'He could be starving, Phoebe. We've got to get him *now*.'

She nodded again, she was so brave, and

I could tell she was thinking, what if Lynne and her giant boyfriend come back? But she said, 'Let's call his name and see if he answers.'

'Rolly! Rolly!' My voice came out high and squeaky, I was so scared, but I think dogs can hear high-pitched sounds better.

But he didn't seem to hear me. Well, he didn't respond. All we could hear was the wind sighing in some far off trees.

I tried calling again.

Still nothing, or – could that sighing sound be a dog whimpering?

We listened again and I thought I heard a yelp.

So did Phoebe. 'Over there! In the corner!'

Phoebe

We charged over the frozen allotment plots to the far corner and as we got nearer the yelps got louder.

'That one!' we gasped together, pointing to a shack made of wooden crates and sheets of corrugated iron. Daisy tried wrenching open the door but it was stronger than it looked – and padlocked!

Rolly was going frantic on the other side.

We tried to comfort him.

'Don't worry, boy. We'll get you out.'

But how?

I pointed at the door hinges, which looked as if they were made of leather. Daisy spotted a spade in one of the plots.

'Out of the way, Rolly! Stand back!'

Between us we managed to hack through one of the hinges, then bend back the door and . . . there was Rolly trembling with joy!

87

Erika

I couldn't believe it when I heard Daisy shouting below my bedroom window.

'We've found him! We've found him!'

And they hadn't just found him, they'd got him.

I looked out of my window and there he was in their arms. My two friends are the bestest friends in the world, and I don't care if Miss Perkins says you can't say bestest. They'd carried Rolly all the way home from these allotments where he'd been hidden, because his paws were so sore he couldn't walk. He must have been trying to escape for days.

Poor Rolly, but he's on the mend now and so am I.

And Rolly's not the only prisoner who's been set free. Ashley is too and his life has changed quite a lot – for the better, I'm glad to say.

In the end the police did find time to investigate and they went round Ashley's house to warn Lynne and her boyfriend that if they ever did anything like that again they'd be in serious trouble. Ashley says Lynne broke down and said she was only trying to help, and then to Ashley's amazement his dad said it was his fault. *His* – I mean – *his dad's*! He actually apologised for putting Ashley under too much pressure.

You may have noticed that I haven't mentioned the Three Counties race. That's because it didn't happen – it was snowed off – but when it's on again Ashley and I are both going to do our very best to win, cheered on by all our friends.

AND, as I've got a few extra days, and can't train anyway, I've agreed to be Magpie in the play.

It's the least I can do for Dais and Phoebe who are THE BEST!